This book belongs to

_____

_____

For Tazzi and Harriet,
with thanks
A.M.

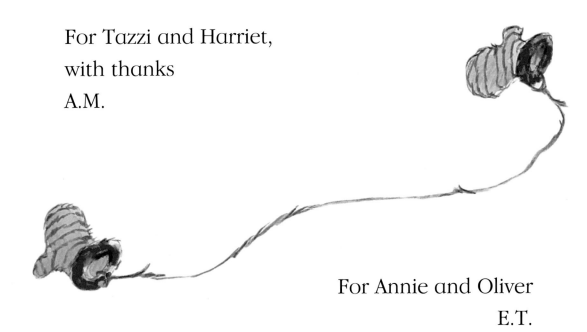

For Annie and Oliver
E.T.

First published in Great Britain in 2005 by Gullane Children's Books
This paperback edition first published 2006 by

Gullane Children's Books,
185 Fleet Street, London EC4A 2HS
www.gullanebooks.com

3   5   7   9   10   8   6   4

Text © Angela McAllister 2005
Illustrations © Eleanor Taylor 2005

ISBN 978-1-86233-592-9

Printed and bound in China

Big Yang
and
Little
Yin

Angela McAllister • Eleanor Taylor

GULLANE
CHILDREN'S BOOKS

Big Yang and Little Yin were playing brave explorers.

"Let's explore the forest," said Little Yin.
"Yes, that's the place for adventures!" said Big Yang.
So Little Yin put her snugly into her trolley, and off they went.

Soon they found a
perfect tree to climb.
Big Yang pulled Little Yin up
onto the lowest branch.
"I want to climb higher,"
said brave Little Yin.

And with Big Yang's help she did.

Then they found a stream.
"Let's make a raft," said Big Yang.
So they turned the trolley upside down.
Big brave Yang paddled the raft round the rocks.

After a while they stopped to pick some berries.
All around, the forest creaked and rustled.
"What's that?" whispered Little Yin.
"Don't worry," said Big Yang.
"There aren't any fierce animals
            in this forest."

"Brave explorers aren't afraid of fierce animals,"
said Little Yin.

Deeper into the woods they went.
Big Yang made them a den.
Dark shadows shifted between the trees.
"Who's there?" whispered Little Yin.
"Don't worry," said Big Yang.
"There aren't any witches in this wood."

"Brave explorers aren't afraid of witches,"
said Little Yin.

Further on, they came to an enormous hollow tree.
Little Yin climbed up and peered into the trunk.

"I think it's a monster's house,"
she said in her explorer's voice.
But suddenly she wobbled and
dropped her snugly inside.

"Don't worry," said Big Yang. "I'll get it for you!"

Big Yang climbed into the
hollow tree and found the snugly.
But he couldn't climb out.

"H

elp!"

cried Big Yang.

Little Yin peeped
through a hole.
"Don't worry," she said.
"I'll get some help."

Little Yin looked around
the deep, dark forest.
"Are you afraid?" asked Big Yang.
"Um . . . brave explorers are never afraid,"
said Little Yin, with a shiver.

Big Yang grabbed his mittens
and threw them out of the tree.
"Take these, Little Yin," he said.
"They'll keep you warm."

Little Yin set off
through the forest.
She came to
Big Yang's den.
Spooky shadows
danced all around.

Suddenly Little Yin
didn't feel brave any more.
She tried to sing a loud,
witch-frightening song,
but her voice was
very small.

In the hollow tree
Big Yang sat alone,
peeping through the hole.

"Maybe this *is*
a monster's house,"
he said to himself,
"and maybe he comes
home for lunch…"

Suddenly Big Yang
didn't feel so brave.
He tried to hum a loud,
monster-scaring hum,
but his voice was
very wobbly.

Little Yin stumbled on until she found the berry bush.
The wind howled through the forest like a fierce animal.
"I don't want to be an explorer any more," said Little Yin.
"I'm only brave with Big Yang to look after me."

But Big Yang was huddled in the hollow tree.
What if Little Yin forgets where to find me! he thought.
Big Yang didn't want to be an explorer any more.
"I'm only brave with Little Yin to look after," he said.

Little Yin sat trembling
in a burrow of leaves.

Then she remembered
Big Yang's mittens.

She put them on.
The mittens were warm
and cosy. Little Yin smiled.
She felt as though Big Yang
was holding her hand.

Up she got.
"I can do it,"
she said bravely.
"I must find help.
Don't worry, Big Yang."
And on she went.

Inside the tree, a teardrop
rolled down Big Yang's cheek.

He picked up the snugly
to wipe his eye.

It was soft and cuddly
and it smelt of Little Yin.
Big Yang smiled.
He felt as if Little Yin
was beside him.

"I'm not really worried,"
said Big Yang bravely.
"Little Yin will
be here soon."
And he practised his
alphabet to cheer himself up.

Before long Little Yin came to the stream and there was her
trolley, still upside down. She had forgotten all about it.
"This is just what we need!" cried Little Yin happily.

When Big Yang heard the
rattling wheels he jumped up.
"Little Yin!" he cried.
"The trolley! How clever!"
"Will it help?" asked Little Yin.
"It's perfect!" said Big Yang.

Big Yang threw the end
of the snugly to Little Yin
and she tied it on to the trolley.

Together they
pushed and pulled
the trolley inside.

Then Big Yang stood on
the trolley, and climbed
out of the hollow tree.

He pulled the trolley
out after him.

"Thank you, Little Yin," said Big Yang, giving her a hug.
"Do you think you know the way home?"
"Oh yes," said Little Yin.
She put the snugly and the mittens
in the trolley and slipped her hand into his.

"Shall we stop for berries on the way?" said Big Yang.
"Yes," said Little Yin.
"Exploring makes you very hungry!"

And with a yawn and a rumble of empty tummies
the two brave friends trundled home.

Other Gullane Children's Books
for you to enjoy . . .

Library Lily

Gillian Shields • illustrated by Francesca Chessa

The only adventures Lily likes are the ones inside her book.
Milly hates to read, but loves to have real adventures.
Could a bookworm and an adventurer become best friends?

Big Bad Wolf Is Good

Simon Puttock • illustrated by Lynne Chapman

Big Bad Wolf has no friends. Is it because he is bad, bad, bad?
"I will be good," he decides. But will the animals trust
a Good Bad Wolf?!

Dog in Boots

Greg Gormley • illustrated by Roberta Angaramo

Puss in Boots has splendid boots – and Dog wants some too!
But will Dog's new footwear be right for digging, scratching,
swimming, and all the other things he loves to do?

Pugwug and Little

Susie Jenkin-Pearce • illustrated by Tina Macnaughton

Pugwug is beside himself with delight when Big Penguin
introduces him to Little. But his new brother – or sister –
doesn't seem to be interested in much! What will it take
to bring Little out of his – or her – shell?